BOB,
SON OF BATTLE

Library of Congress Cataloging in Publication Data

Hinkle, Don.
　Bob, son of Battle.

　Summary: Two sheep farmers and their sheepdogs
engage in a years-long battle to prove their
superiority in handling sheep—a battle which must
end in death.
　1. Dogs—Juvenile literature.　[1. Dogs—Fiction]
I. Riccio, Frank, ill.　II. Ollivant, Alfred, 1874-1927.
Bob, son of Battle.　III. Title.
PZ10.3.052Bo　1988　[Fic]　87-15477
ISBN 0-8167-1211-5 (lib. bdg.)
ISBN 0-8167-1212-3 (pbk.)

BOB, SON OF BATTLE

Alfred Ollivant

Retold by
Don Hinkle

Illustrated by
Frank Riccio and Doron Ben-Ami

Troll Associates

The sheep country of northern Britain is lonely. Only a few sheep farms and small villages break up the miles of bleak moors and ravines. Here, most men talk— if at all—about sheep and their sheepdogs.

A sheep farmer without a sheepdog is like a ship without a rudder. Between farmer and dog exists a special bond— and an unwritten law. Sheep farmers teach their dogs from the moment they're born that any sheepdog who kills a sheep will itself be killed. It is the one unforgivable crime a sheepdog could commit.

In contrast, the one great victory any dog could achieve is to win the Shepherds Trophy at the Champion Challenge Dale Cup contest held each summer. It is the most important event of the year in the region. For many years, the famous Gray Dogs of Kenmuir won this prize. They were raised by the Moore family at Kenmuir Farm.

The last of the famous Gray Dogs of Kenmuir was Bob.
He was the son of Battle, a Shepherds Trophy winner many
times before. Bob's coat was dark gray, splashed with lighter
touches. His chest was pure white, and the top of his head
was sprinkled with white. He was small, fast, agile, and
strong. And yet he was gentle. The young dog coaxed the
sheep instead of bullying them. Bob did his work so well that
it amazed even his master, James Moore.

There was one man, however, who had no admiration for Bob. He was Adam M'Adam, a small man with a bitter face who lived on Grange Farm. He was a loner who drank too much and he had nothing good to say about his neighbors. There was hardly a man in the land who had not felt the sting of his sharp tongue. He had not one friend in the village.

Even his young son, David, couldn't love him. In fact, the boy spent more time at Kenmuir than in his own house, especially in the company of the Moores' daughter, Maggie. David thought of James and Elizabeth Moore as his real parents. Adam M'Adam bitterly resented that, beating the boy with a leather strap at any excuse.

M'Adam owned a vicious dog called Red Wull. He cared more for this dog than for his own son. In turn, Red Wull adored his master and hated the son.

Red Wull was an immense dog with a stubby tail. He had a large bull head with cropped ears. His savage face held menacing, gleaming eyes. Red Wull's powerful jaws had killed several dogs in the town and wounded many others. Even men feared his deadly throat-grip. They said of Red Wull that he was "quick as a cat, with the heart of a lion and an ugly temper." Because Adam M'Adam especially hated James Moore, Red Wull hated Moore's dog, Bob.

As a sheepdog, Red Wull was second only to Bob. M'Adam constantly trained his Wullie, hoping he'd become better than Bob and thus the best dog in the land. He would say, "Well done, Wullie! Well done!" Then the dog would place his front paws on the man's shoulders, stand with his great head over his master's, and wag his stump tail.

One terrible winter the snow piled up in thick, billowy drifts. Hundreds of sheep, trying to find shelter in protected spots, were buried and lost. More than one man and many a dog lost their lives while quietly doing their duty. They slid to their deaths over slippery ledges or were smothered beneath avalanches.

Two men, each with his shaggy companion, braved even the worst storms: Adam M'Adam with Red Wull, and James Moore with Bob. Between them, they lost fewer sheep than any farmer in the area.

During this same winter, another daughter was born to Elizabeth Moore. But Elizabeth died during childbirth. James and Maggie were stricken with grief, and David M'Adam felt he had lost a second mother.

The funeral took place on a gray, overcast day. Getting ready for it, David took his father's new coat without thinking. Adam M'Adam saw his son leave with the coat. Angry, he stormed after David to stop him. But then, Adam heard the distant toll of the church bell. Suddenly, he remembered his own wife's death.

Adam M'Adam ran to his room. He dropped to his knees as he searched through a great wooden chest. He finally found a paper packet wrapped with a yellow ribbon. Inside the packet was a heart-shaped frame holding a photograph. The face—a sweet, laughing face—looked up at him.

A tender smile crept over M'Adam's face. Memories flooded back to a day some years ago. "Put the child on my bed," Flora had said weakly to her husband, Adam. "I must bid my final goodbye to you and him."

Tiny David called, "You're not going away, are you, Mother? Don't leave me."

"Yes, David. Away." She tried to smile.

"Take me with you, Mother!" David put his arms about her neck and sobbed.

Flora turned her head to her husband and whispered, "Adam, you'll have to be mother and father to the boy now."

"I will! I swear I will!" he declared. Then with a look of peace on her face, Flora died.

The memory of Flora's death was as strong as ever for Adam. He was still on his knees when he heard his son returning from the funeral for Elizabeth Moore. Adam recalled Flora's last words to him. He knew he hadn't kept his word. But it can't be too late, he thought. I'll humble myself before David, and I *will* be mother and father to him now.

Adam rose from his knees when he heard the front door shut. "David!" the little man called in a trembling voice. "I've something to say to you!"

The boy burst into the room. His face was stained with tears and rain. His father's coat was wet and dirty. On the way home, he had flung himself down on the ground, weeping for his second mother. "What do you want?" he asked angrily, expecting only the worst from his father.

Adam M'Adam looked at the picture of his dead wife. "I'd like to say...I've been thinking...I think I should tell you...it's not an easy thing for a man to say."

He looked at David, hoping the boy could understand what he was trying to say. But his glance rested upon his coat. David mistook his father's look and the tremor in his voice.

"Here! Take your coat!" He tore it off, flung it at his father's feet, and charged out of the room.

M'Adam looked at the wet coat lying in a bundle at his feet. "Did you hear him, Wullie?" The dog's stump tail wagged from habit. Red Wull was always glad when father and son quarreled.

A bitter smile crept across Adam M'Adam's face. He looked again at the picture of his wife. "You cannot say I didn't try. And you cannot expect me to try again," he muttered. He slipped the photograph into his pocket. Then he went out into the gloomy drizzle, still smiling bitterly.

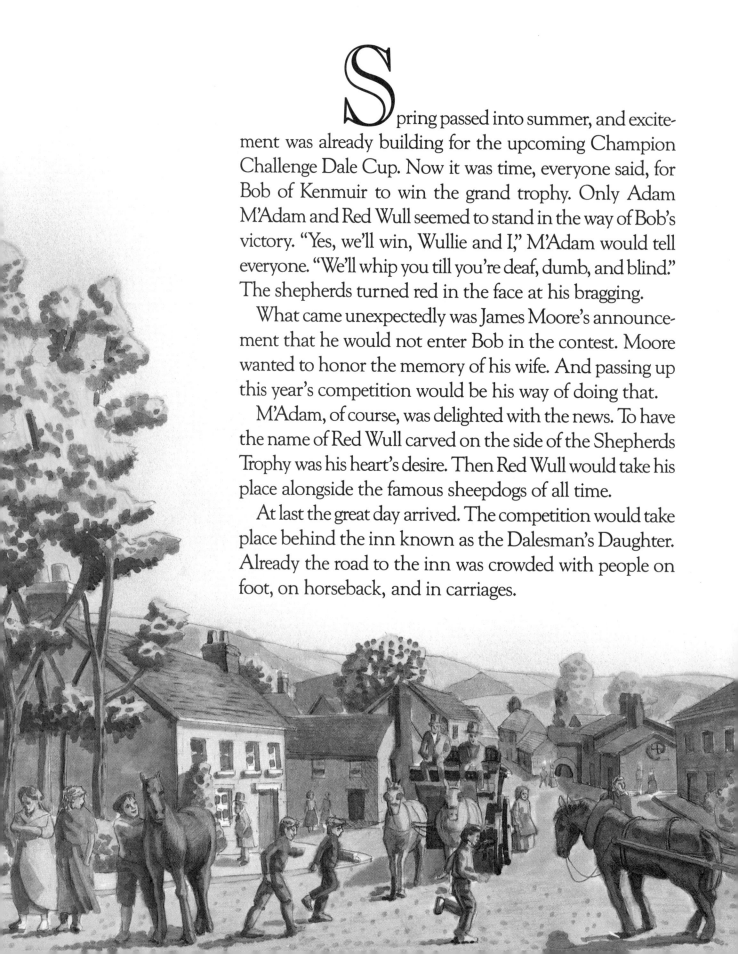

Spring passed into summer, and excitement was already building for the upcoming Champion Challenge Dale Cup. Now it was time, everyone said, for Bob of Kenmuir to win the grand trophy. Only Adam M'Adam and Red Wull seemed to stand in the way of Bob's victory. "Yes, we'll win, Wullie and I," M'Adam would tell everyone. "We'll whip you till you're deaf, dumb, and blind." The shepherds turned red in the face at his bragging.

What came unexpectedly was James Moore's announcement that he would not enter Bob in the contest. Moore wanted to honor the memory of his wife. And passing up this year's competition would be his way of doing that.

M'Adam, of course, was delighted with the news. To have the name of Red Wull carved on the side of the Shepherds Trophy was his heart's desire. Then Red Wull would take his place alongside the famous sheepdogs of all time.

At last the great day arrived. The competition would take place behind the inn known as the Dalesman's Daughter. Already the road to the inn was crowded with people on foot, on horseback, and in carriages.

The rules of the contest were simple: Each shepherd and dog must gather three scattered sheep, herd them through a marked course, and pen them in sight of all the onlookers.

When Red Wull came out to herd his sheep through the course, he did not wait or coax them. Instead, he drove and forced them on. He moved his sheep along at a rapid rate. Still he never missed a turn, never faltered.

There were not many people in the audience who really respected M'Adam and his dog. Only a smattering of applause could be heard when Red Wull won and the Squire's wife handed over the shiny cup.

"Mr. M'Adam, I present you with the Shepherds Trophy. Keep it, guard it, and love it as your own. Win it again if you can. Twice more in a row, and it's yours."

M'Adam took the trophy tenderly. "It shall not leave my house, your ladyship, if Wullie and I can help it."

Adam M'Adam went home and placed the cup on the kitchen mantel, just below an old bell-mouthed shoulder gun that hung on the wall. M'Adam spent his moments shining the trophy. "See, Wullie! She shines like a twinkle in the sky." M'Adam was so happy that he even forgot about his hatred for James Moore.

But one day he overheard David reading aloud the long list of Shepherds Trophy winners. Nearly all of them were Gray Dogs owned by the Moore family. Then David came to the last name on the list. "M'Adam's Red Wull," David read with contempt. He ran his thumb across the name, as though to wipe it away.

Adam M'Adam burst into the room. "So," he cried, "you're praying that James Moore will win the cup away from your own dad! You can't touch my trophy! Go see James Moore and his worthless mutt."

"Okay," his son replied. "Shall I take the cup with me to give them? Or will you wait till they take it away from you?"

M'Adam's jealousy blazed. He had won the Shepherds Trophy once. He had sworn he would win it again!

The conflicts between this father and son, between Adam M'Adam and James Moore, and between Bob and Red Wull soon became obvious to everyone. People started to whisper. "M'Adam's gone mad," said one man. "He'll stop at nothing!" Another man added, "No, not even murder!"

Not long afterward, in the middle of the night, James Moore was awakened by a low moaning outside his farmhouse. He ran to the window to see Bob dragging himself across the moonlit yard. His head was down, his proud tail lowered, his legs heavy. Moore ran downstairs. Bob struggled to reach him, could not, and fell, whimpering. Bob's tongue was swollen and almost black. His breathing was slow, and his body twitched. Even his soft gray eyes were bloodshot.

For the rest of the night and well into morning, James Moore stayed with Bob and helped save his life. There were moments during the night, however, when Moore thought the best sheepdog in the region would not live to see sunrise. But he did, barely, and in the next few weeks both James Moore and Maggie nursed Bob back to health. They knew he had been poisoned, and they immediately suspected Adam M'Adam. But they had no proof.

When the next Champion Challenge Dale Cup contest took place, Bob won. His expert driving and penning were admired by crowd and competitors alike. Bob was patient yet persistent, firmly coaxing his sheep all the way. So the Shepherds Trophy was won again by a Gray Dog of Kenmuir. Bob trotted proudly alongside James Moore as the crowd cheered.

Along on the far bank of the stream stood Adam M'Adam and Red Wull. As Adam listened to the cheers, his face twisted in self-pity while Red Wull snorted defiantly. David had also cheered for Bob. The little man whispered, "He's happy. They're all happy, not because James Moore won but because you and I were beaten, Wullie. They're all against us. It's you and I alone, Wullie, against the world!"

When the time came for the trophy to be awarded to James Moore, Adam M'Adam would not return it. The crowd turned ugly and started toward him, but Red Wull guarded the thin plank bridge after M'Adam crossed the stream. Only one man at a time could cross over the bridge, and none dared do it against that ferocious dog. M'Adam sneered at them, then turned and walked slowly away. Once he was a safe distance from the angry crowd, he called Red Wull to follow.

All the next day, Adam M'Adam sat beneath the trophy with a bottle in his hands, and Red Wull at his feet. Toward evening the little man rose and took the cup from its place of honor, then sat with it in his arms. He hugged it, crying and rocking back and forth. Red Wull sat up on his haunches and weaved from side to side.

"We won her, Wullie, you and I. We won her fair. She's lit the house for us, and is the only thing we have to look at and love. Now they're taking her away, and it will be night again." Adam M'Adam's voice rose high. "Did they win her fair, Wullie? No! They plotted and they beat us. And now they're robbing us! But they shall not have her. She's ours or nobody's, Wullie!"

Suddenly, Adam rushed outside. In a moment he returned, carrying a large ax. He swung the ax at the Shepherds Trophy—and missed. The ax blade sank into the

wooden table. He tugged and strained, trying to pull out the ax so he could strike again. But the handle snapped, and he tottered back as the table toppled over. The cup fell to the floor. Horrified that he had nearly destroyed his prize possession, Adam M'Adam ran from the house.

When he returned that night, the cup was gone. M'Adam screamed and beat on the walls. Then he grew deadly calm. He sat at the table, staring at the door and waiting for his son.

David had been visiting Maggie Moore, whom he hoped to marry someday soon. When he walked through the door of his home, David found his father facing him.

"Was it you who took my cup?" the father asked.

"I took *Mr. Moore's* cup," the boy replied.

M'Adam drew himself up to his full height. "James Moore put you up to it! He doesn't dare come himself. So he sent the boy to rob the father. He's afraid of me."

"Mr. Moore had nothing to do with it," David said. "I'm no thief! I gave to the man only what my father wrongfully kept from him. If there's a thief here, it's you."

At this, Adam M'Adam grabbed the leather strap from its hook and whipped it across his son's shoulders. As he did so, Adam whistled to his dog. "Wullie! Wullie! Come here, boy!"

When David felt the strap across his back, he ran toward the open door. Again M'Adam lashed him and cried, "Quick, Wullie! Come quick!" David shut the door just before Red Wull got there.

After striking David again with the strap, Adam leaped to the old gun on the wall. But David pushed his father so that the man staggered back, dropping the strap. Outside, Red Wull whined and scratched at the closed door. With fury in his eyes, David lunged at his father. Suddenly, frightened, M'Adam reached in his pocket, pulled out something, and flung it on the table. David looked down and saw a photograph. It was his mother's face gazing up at him!

"Mother!" he sobbed. "Mother! You saved him—and me!"

Some minutes passed before David could move. Then he took some sheep shears off the wall and, still trembling, began cutting the leather strap into little pieces. "There! And there! And there!" David said with each snip. Then he turned and looked at his father. "If you ever hit me again, there may be no one to save you!"

A year later, Bob won the Shepherds Trophy for a second time. But the next few days of celebration ended abruptly for James Moore as he was walking through the fields one dark night. Close by were some sheep huddled together in fear. Curious, Moore walked over to them. In their midst was a dead sheep. Its throat had been torn open.

This was the first of what became a long string of sheep killings. In the market and in the neighboring village, the conversation was always about the latest sheep killing—and which dog was doing it. The killer always struck on dark nights, and soon the villagers were calling him the Black Killer. Hardly a farm in the countryside escaped having its sheep slain—except Kenmuir Farm and Grange Farm.

One morning in late spring, David rose early. Going to the window, he saw Red Wull bounding up the hill. His flanks were splashed with red mud, his tongue lolled out, and foam dripped from his jaws. It seemed as if he had come far and fast. Red Wull crept into the house through an open back window.

David dressed quickly. As he headed out the door, a photograph fell from his pocket. It was a picture of Maggie Moore. Seeing the photo drop, Adam M'Adam grabbed it.

"Hee, hee, hee, Wullie, what's this?" Adam asked. He held the photograph close. "Hee, hee, hee! Why, it's the girl who's distracting my Davie from his duties to his father!"

"Give it to me!" David ordered fiercely. "It's mine!"

"No, no. It's my duty as your dear dad to keep you from such a girl." He threw the photograph to the dog. "Tear her, Wullie!"

David seized his father by the shoulders. "I'll go away," he shouted, "and leave you and your Wullie!"

The little man burst into artificial tears, his face in his hands. "Oh, Wullie, he's going to leave us! Oh, my little Davie! He's going away!"

David began walking down the hill, then turned. "A word of warning," he shouted. "Keep a close eye on your Wullie's comings and goings, especially at nights. Or you may wake to a surprise one morning."

In an instant, Adam M'Adam stopped his pretended sorrow. "And why do you say that?"

"This morning I saw your Wullie galloping up the hill, all foaming and red-splashed. What had he been up to, I'd like to know?"

"What should he be doing, but watching my flocks? Especially when the Black Killer might be out wandering."

David laughed harshly. "Yes, the Black Killer was out, I'll bet. And you may hear about it before evening." With that, David turned and left.

When nightfall came, David returned to the Grange. As he entered the house, the thin raspy voice of Adam broke the quiet. "Would you oblige me, sir, by lighting the lamp? Or would that soil your dainty fingers?"

David lit the lamp and said, "Another sheep was lost to the Black Killer last night."

Adam rose to his feet. "So what?"

"Your Wullie was out last night."

"Go on."

"Now everyone knows that your Wullie is the Black Killer."

"Wullie!" Adam called.

The dog leaped with a roar, but David gave him a mighty kick on the jaw. Red Wull howled in pain. Then David gripped his father around the waist and lifted him. Adam flailed his arms at his son's face.

"Black Killer!" shouted Adam. "I'll tell you who the Black Killer is. He lives at Kenmuir!"

Then David dropped Adam. He fell with a groan.

Suddenly, the lamp went out. In the darkness and silence, David stood panting. Something was creeping closer to him. "Father, are you hurt?" he whispered.

Without warning, a great body struck David on the chest. A hot breath hit his face. Defending himself, David gripped a hairy throat. Then he lifted the huge body of Red Wull and heaved it away from him. It struck the wall and fell with a soft thud.

Before David could get his balance, a hand grabbed his ankle to trip him. David kicked with all his strength. Another awful groan rose in the darkness as David staggered against the door and ran out.

Outside, a great fear gripped David. He crept back to the kitchen door and listened. Then he opened it a crack. Not a sound could be heard inside. David banged the door shut. Fearing he had seriously hurt his father, he turned and plunged into the night, fleeing through the blackness.

The following Saturday, Adam M'Adam appeared in a local inn. One arm was in a sling, and his head was bandaged. "I was sitting in my chair, asleep," he said to anyone who'd listen, "when David crept up behind and leaped on my back. I knew nothing till I found myself on the floor and him kneeling on me. I could see he was set on killing me, so I said, 'Do your worst, foul assassin!' And he tried. It was a brutal assault on an old man by his son! That will look noble in the papers, hee, hee! They won't let him off without two years in jail. And I doubt if that Maggie Moore will wait for him that long!"

26

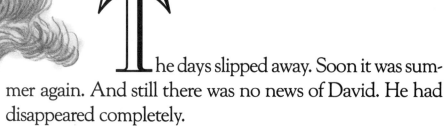

The days slipped away. Soon it was summer again. And still there was no news of David. He had disappeared completely.

Maggie Moore no longer sang at her work. The cheer was gone from her face. Even the upcoming Champion Challenge Dale Cup contest did not hold the same interest for her. She knew Bob had a chance to win the Shepherds Trophy outright if he could win this third time. But her thoughts were on David.

There was not a cloud in the sky when the big day finally came. The weather was calm and beautiful. From all around the region, people came to see whether the famous Gray Dog of Kenmuir could win the Shepherds Trophy permanently. Bob held his dark head high as he watched his challengers. Dog after dog ran the course. All did well.

Then it was Bob's turn. The crowd was silent. Bob quickly herded his three sheep around the first flag. One bright-eyed sheep made a dash, but Bob quickly brought him back to the small flock. Down the slope they came toward a gap in a wall where James Moore stood. Bob worked the sheep patiently, never hurrying them yet bringing them along at a good pace. Not a word was spoken and barely a gesture made as the sheep moved through the gap and along the hill next to the spectators. They made a wide sweep for the turn at the flags and headed for the bridge.

"Steady," whispered the crowd.

Close to the bridge, the three sheep dashed apart. Again Bob pulled them together and coaxed them, a step at a time, toward the narrow bridge. One sheep started across, and the others followed.

In the middle of the bridge, however, the leader stopped. Time was flying. Many spectators eyed their watches nervously. "We're beaten. We're beaten," sobbed more than one onlooker who had bet on Bob. Just then, Bob leaped on the back of the last sheep. It surged forward and pushed the next, which pushed the leader. Soon all three were across and climbing the slope toward the pen.

The crowd hurrahed but then fell silent again. At the pen, James Moore, his face determined, herded the sheep in. Bob, his eyes big and bright, dropped, crawled, and crept closer and closer until the last sheep reluctantly passed through— on the stroke of time.

A roar went up from the crowd. "If only David were here to see it!" Maggie Moore said, feeling happy and sad at the same time. The spectators surged forward, but the guards kept them back.

"Back, please! Don't push!" urged the guards. "M'Adam's turn is next!"

From the far bank, M'Adam watched the scene. His coat and cap were off, and his hair gleamed white in the sun.

"Now, Wullie, now or never!" he commanded.

Red Wull was after his sheep, starting off with a rush. Up the slope the sheep ran, around the first flag, already galloping. Down the hill for the gap they swept, ears back, feet flying. After them scurried Red Wull. And last of all, leaping over the ground, was M'Adam. From behind he urged Red Wull to herd the sheep even faster than Bob had.

Red Wull raced parallel to the sheep and above them. All four were traveling at a rapid speed. The two flags were barely twenty yards in front of them.

"Turn them, Wullie!" shouted M'Adam from behind.

The great dog swerved down on the flying three. They turned and dropped between the flags and raced toward the stream. From the crowd came a small burst of applause. The leading sheep galloped right onto the center of the bridge— and abruptly stopped. The crowd was instantly silent. Red Wull tried to imitate Bob. He leaped onto the back of the last sheep. But Red Wull was so heavy that the sheep staggered, slipped, and fell into the stream.

"He's lost it now," someone groaned quietly.

The struggling sheep might have drowned, but M'Adam jumped into the water and lifted it onto the bank. Then he

scrambled forward and raced after sheep and dog. M'Adam's face was white, and he gasped for breath. Trembling in every limb, he was determined to finish the course.

At the pen, the crowd stared silently as M'Adam tapped with his stick on the ground, coaxing the sheep in. Red Wull, his tongue out and flanks heaving, crept and crawled up to the opening, patient as he had never been before. The sheep were in—and in a time very close to Bob's. There was a lukewarm, half-hearted cheer, then silence.

Exhausted and still shaking, M'Adam and Red Wull stood waiting. Nearby, James Moore and Bob also stood waiting. The judges were comparing their notes. Then one of the judges went up to James Moore and shook his hand. The handshake signaled victory. There was a loud cry from the crowd.

To Adam M'Adam, standing with his back to the crowd, the wild cheering announced defeat. "We might have known it, Wullie," he muttered. M'Adam and Red Wull glumly headed back to Grange Farm.

With the Shepherds Trophy theirs to keep now, James Moore and Bob returned to Kenmuir Farm. But the joy James Moore felt did not last long. Less than a week went by before he was awakened one night by a whimpering cry beneath his window. Looking out, James saw it was Bob.

There was a deep gash in his throat. Red stained the white on his chest, and his head and neck were clotted with blood.

As James doctored him tenderly, he found a cluster of tawny red hair in the corners of Bob's bloody lips. He was relieved that the dog's wounds proved less severe than they looked. Bob's gray coat, thick about his throat, had saved him.

After his wounds were washed and bandaged, Bob jumped from the table and rushed for the door. He led Moore to the pasture where a murdered sheep lay. The signs of a terrible struggle were all around. The earth was torn up and patches of grass were uprooted. Here and there, ringlets of wool and tufts of tawny hair mingled with iron-gray wisps.

James Moore stooped and picked up something. "The Black Killer has claimed his last sheep," he muttered. He strode away up the hill, with Bob at his heels.

Adam M'Adam was standing in his doorway. As James Moore and Bob passed through the gap in the hedge, M'Adam cried, "James Moore!" with both hands extended, as though welcoming a long-lost brother. "It's a long time since you've honored my poor house!"

"One of my sheep has been killed," James Moore said.

"By the Black Killer?"

"By the Black Killer."

"Dear, dear! It's come to that, has it?" Adam's eyes wandered to Bob. "Poor dog!" Then brightening, he asked, "You've come to borrow my gun?"

"You fool, M'Adam," replied Moore angrily. "Did you ever hear of a sheepdog killing his master's sheep?"

The little man shouldered up to his tall enemy. "If not him, who then?" Adam asked, daring him to reply.

James Moore's eyebrows lowered. "Your Red Wull, M'Adam. Your Wull's the Black Killer!"

"You lie! You lie!" M'Adam cried in a dreadful scream. "Your own dog's done it, and now you hope to throw the blame on my Wullie. Where's your proof?"

James Moore held out his right hand. "Here's proof enough for you, M'Adam."

"Where?"

M'Adam bent to look closer. In Moore's palm was a clump of tawny red hair. Adam M'Adam spat deliberately into the upturned palm. "That's for your proof!"

Just then, Red Wull limped around the corner of the house. His head and neck were swathed in bandages. The huge dog stopped abruptly. His hackles rose up, each hair standing on end, till his whole body resembled a newly cut wheatfield. Red Wull trotted forward heavily, his head sinking lower as he came.

Bob, eager to renew the battle, went to meet Red Wull. Confidently, Bob picked his way across the yard, head and tail erect. But the two men called off their dogs and would

34

not let them resume the fight they'd had near the dead sheep.

Then M'Adam spoke. "I'll tell you the truth," he said slowly. "I was up this morning, and I saw a dog creep up to the sheep on the hillside and kill one. The sun was shining by then, and I saw the dog as clearly as I see you now. It was that dog there," he cried, pointing an accusing finger at Bob. "I swear it!" His voice rose as he went on. "Wullie went after him. They fought until I ran over. Then your dog left for Kenmuir, and Wullie came up the hill to me. It's the truth I'm telling you. Take him home, James Moore, and let his dinner be an ounce of lead shot."

M'Adam spoke with a strong belief in his own story that might have convinced anyone who didn't know him as well. But James Moore looked at him with scorn.

"Today's Monday," said Moore. "I give you till Saturday. If you haven't done your duty by then, I shall come do it for you, M'Adam."

As Moore turned away, M'Adam sprang after him and clutched his arm. "Look here, James Moore!" he cried. "You're big and I'm small. You're strong and I'm weak. You have everyone on your side. I have no one—not even a son. You tell your story, and they'll probably believe you. I'll tell mine, and they'll think I lie. But if I ever catch you on my land again, I swear I'll not spare you!"

Two nights later, James Moore was crossing a stream in a furious storm, coming home from a meeting at the inn. Wet and weary, he plodded on, wondering whether Maggie would be up and whether Bob would come out to meet him.

Almost overcome by the storm, he reached high ground and rested. As he lay there panting, the moon gleamed down through a gap in the fast-moving clouds. James Moore froze at what he saw. It was a flock of motionless sheep, staring with frightened eyes. Beyond the flock was a boulder casting a long shadow in the moonlight. Beneath it were two dark figures, one struggling feebly.

Moore crawled toward the trembling sheep. The moon flung off its veil of cloud. A short distance away was the boulder. Near its shadow lay a dead sheep. And standing beside the sheep, his coat all ruffled by the storm, was Bob of Kenmuir. The silver moon gleamed on him. Then the moon slipped behind the clouds again.

In the darkness, James Moore, lying with his face pressed downward, moaned like a man in great pain. Then he heard a small laugh. A little man, wet and shrunken, sat hunched on a mound above. He was rocking his shriveled form back and forth.

"Hee, hee, and didn't I tell you your dog is the Black Killer, James Moore?" asked Adam M'Adam.

James Moore rose to his feet and stumbled toward M'Adam. All of a sudden, someone else's hand caught James by the shoulder.

"Mr. Moore! Look!" It was the voice of David M'Adam. He had returned. David lifted his hand and pointed. Moore turned and looked.

There in the moonlight was Bob and the murdered sheep. Suddenly, a shadow near the boulder moved! It was the Black Killer at his feast.

Adam M'Adam's voice pierced the silence. "Ah, Wullie!" It was the voice of a man whose heart was breaking.

For the only time in his life, Red Wull became afraid. He crouched down upon the ground. A cry like that of a lost soul rose up from him. It floated on the still night air—a long sad wail.

"Wullie, Wullie, come to me!" said Adam M'Adam.

The huge brute came crawling toward him on his belly, whimpering as he came. Red Wull knew his fate. But that wasn't what troubled him. His real pain was that he had betrayed his master's trust.

"Wullie, my Wullie!" Adam said very gently. "A man's wife, a man's son, a man's dog! They're all I've ever had. And now each of them is lost to me! I am alone!"

Red Wull raised himself and placed his forepaws on his master's chest tenderly. The great dog did not want to hurt his master, who was already hurt past healing. Red Wull towered above him, while Adam laid his two cold hands on the dog's back.

Quietly, Bob moved to stand near James Moore and David M'Adam.

"Should I go to him?" David asked hoarsely, nodding toward his father.

"No, lad," James Moore replied. "It's time you came home to see Maggie."

The following morning, there was a sheep auction on the sandy floor of the Dalesman's Daughter parlor. Adam M'Adam sat in his chair with a vacant look on his face.

Each man who came in and saw Adam asked others about him while their dogs sniffed about. One dog walked quietly to the back door of the inn and looked out. On the slope below him he saw Red Wull stalking up and down, gaunt and grim, like a prisoner awaiting sentence. The dog walked back to where the other dogs were, going to each one as though urging him on to some great task.

All the while, Adam M'Adam sat as though he neither heard nor saw. He seemed lost in a dream. He hardly noticed the other dogs pattering out of the inn. They dropped down the slope—determined to end the bloody reign of the Black Killer once and for all.

Red Wull saw them coming. He was glad. His great head was held high as he dared them to come on. And on they came, moving slowly and silently. The sheepdogs walked around Red Wull on their toes, stiff and short like cats on coals. Their backs were humped and their heads averted. Yet each was eyeing Red Wull, seeking a spot to attack.

Red Wull remained still, his great chin cocked with a dreadful grin. When the sheepdogs had him completely surrounded, they struck like lightning.

The great brute rolled over and over and up again. Leaping here, striking there, shaking himself free, he fought with paws and body and teeth. More than once he broke right through the pack, only to turn again and face it. Up and down the slope Red Wull tossed, leaving everywhere a trail of red. Here and there a dog lay grinning with a clutch of tawny hair and flesh in its teeth.

Suddenly, Red Wull rose up. He reared to his full height, with his head ragged and bleeding. Down he went again, smothered beneath the weight of numbers. Yet he struggled up again. He sobbed as he fiercely fought on.

It could not last. Down he went. The battle had all but ended.

"Wullie, my Wullie!" screamed M'Adam, running down the slope toward the battle scene. "Wullie! Wullie! Come to me!"

At his shrill cry, a gigantic figure, tawny and red, fought to the surface. Red Wull struggled toward his master, dragging the pack behind him.

"Wullie! Wullie!"

The pack clung to him. They were all about him. Then down he went again with a sob.

The men started pulling off the dead and living dogs. At the bottom lay Red Wull. Adam M'Adam sat down and took Red Wull in his lap very tenderly.

"They've killed you at last, Wullie," he said quietly. He sat swaying back and forth, talking to the dead dog at his feet. No one disturbed him.

It was long past noon when M'Adam laid Red Wull gently down and walked toward the plank bridge. It was the bridge Red Wull had once held against a hundred. M'Adam crossed it and turned. "Wullie!" he cried. "Wullie! Come to me, boy!" He waited a while. "Aren't you coming, Wullie?" he asked.

Adam walked back and stooped over the dead dog. Lovingly, he raised it in his arms, slung the great body on his back, and staggered away. The limp carcass hung from the little man's shoulders.

Next day, they found Adam M'Adam and his Red Wull together in death. The dog was lying next to the boulder where, as the Black Killer, he had slain his last. Close by, Adam M'Adam's dim, dead eyes stared up at the heavens. One hand was still clasping the crumpled photograph of his wife. His small, weary body was finally at rest. His face—mocking no longer—had a peaceful look.

Adam M'Adam and Red Wull were buried not far from each other. The only mourners were David M'Adam, James and Maggie Moore, and—standing off at a distance—Bob.

The last and best of the famous Gray Dogs of Kenmuir lived out his days in glory. As time passed, men spoke of Bob as the finest sheepdog ever to have lived in the region.